RHYS AND THE CUCKOO OF RISCA

Story: Siân Lewis
Illustrations: Gini Wade

'Sun, sun, come out to play,' said Rhys.
Rhys lived in Risca.
All summer long he liked to watch the bright
warm sun climb over the hill.
Then one day . . .

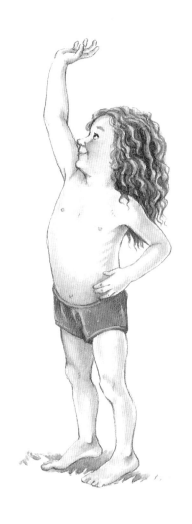

. . . the sun didn't come.
Rhys was rolling around in the autumn leaves.
'Dad,' he said. 'Where's the sun gone?'
'Oh!' said Dad with a shake of his head.
'The sun has gone away.
It's flown off with the cuckoo.'

Winter came to Risca and big white flakes
of snow fell softly from the sky.
Rhys went out to build a snowman in the garden.
'Mam,' he said. 'Will the sun ever come back?'
'Oh yes,' said Mam. 'One day the sun will
come back with the cuckoo.'

At last the wind blew the snow away.
It tickled the spring leaves on the trees.
Rhys was busy picking dandelions
in the hedge.

He'd forgotten all about the sun, till . . .
'Cuckoo!'
A grey bird landed on the tree above his head.
'Mam! Dad!' called Rhys.
Mam and Dad ran out of the house.
'Cuckoo,' sang the grey bird —
and a smiling face peeped over the hill.
The cuckoo had brought the sun back to Risca.

In Risca doors and windows opened wide.
Everyone rushed out into the garden.
Rhys helped Mam and Dad to plant potatoes,
carrots, peas and beans.
The sun shone down and warmed the rain
to make the seeds grow.

'Thank you for bringing us the sun, Cuckoo,' said Mam.

'We have such a good time in the sun. We can sit out in the garden and pick all sorts of fruit and vegetables.'

'And I can play in the water,' said Rhys, jumping into his tub

— Splish! Splash!

One day, when Rhys was picking potatoes with
Mam, he saw the sun sit down on top of the hill.
'Mam,' said Rhys.
'What's the matter with the sun?'
'Oh,' said Mam. 'The sun is getting ready
to fly away again with the cuckoo.'
'What a shame!' said Dad.

'What a great shame!'
said the people of Risca.
They all came into Rhys's garden.
'We must stop the cuckoo flying away,' said one.
'Yes,' said another. 'Let's build a high high hedge
all around Risca.'

The people went up into the woods.
They hewed and chopped
and built a high high hedge.
The sun peeped over the top
and looked down in surprise.
It was looking for the cuckoo.
'The cuckoo's staying with us,' called the people
of Risca.
'It can't fly over the hedge.'

'Cuckoo-oo-oo,' chuckled a small voice.
'Cuckoo-cuckoo,' sang the cuckoo
in the tree above Rhys.
But Rhys wasn't listening.
He was watching the pale weak sun.
It was slipping down the hedge.
'Oh!' he cried. 'The sun is going to fall.
What can we do?'
'Cuckoo-oo-ooo,' chuckled the cuckoo out loud.

Then she spread her wings
and rose up in the air.
Up and up she flew
higher than the people,
higher than the houses,
higher than the trees.
'Cuckoo-cuckoo.'
With no trouble at all, the cuckoo
flew over the high high hedge.
She caught the tired sun in her beak
and carried it away from Risca.

'Oh!' said Mam and Dad.
'Oh!' grumbled the people of Risca.
'How can we enjoy ourselves
when there's no sun in the sky?'
'Easy,' said Rhys with a big smile.
'We can roll in the autumn leaves.
We can play in the soft white snow.
We can pick dandelions in the hedge.
And then . . .

Next year the cuckoo'll bring the sun back to Risca.'